THE WAR OF THE WORLDS

H. G. WELLS

REAL READS

D0190786

www.realreads.co.uk

Retold by Eric Brown
Illustrated by Felix Bennett

Published by Real Reads Ltd
Stroud, Gloucestershire, UK
www.realreads.co.uk

First published in 2008
Reprinted 2011

ISBN 978-1-906230-12-8

Printed in China by Wai Man Book Binding (China) Ltd
Designed by Lucy Guenot
Typeset by Bookcraft Ltd, Stroud, Gloucestershire

CONTENTS

THE CHARACTERS

The narrator

The narrator witnesses a Martian invasion. Can he escape their aggression? Will his life ever be the same again?

The narrator's wife

The narrator's wife flees to the nearby town of Leatherhead, but is that far enough? Will they ever see each other again?

The curate

The curate is a terrified man. Will his fear put both him and the narrator in even greater danger?

The artilleryman

The artilleryman is a fine
soldier. Can the human race
depend upon such men to
defeat the invaders?

Ogilvy

Ogilvy is one of the first men
to greet the Martians. Will he
live to tell the tale?

The Martians

Escaping their own dying
planet, the Martians want
to settle on earth. Can they
live in harmony with us,
or must the human race
fight to survive? How
do you kill a Martian?

THE WAR OF THE WORLDS

No one would have believed at the end of
the nineteenth century that planet earth was
being watched by beings more intelligent than
humankind, who regarded our planet with envy
and were drawing up plans against us. The
planet Mars, I will remind you, orbits the sun at a
distance of one hundred and forty million miles.
It has air and water and all that is necessary
to support life. And yet over the millennia the
planet has cooled, its air has thinned, and its
oceans diminished. Mars is a slowly dying world.
The Martians, gazing acquisitively across the
gulf of space, watched our own warm and watery
planet – and planned invasion.

One night six years ago, astronomers on
earth beheld a huge explosion of gas upon the
surface of Mars. Their instruments indicated a
mass of flame moving towards the earth at great

speed. The newspapers paid little attention, so most people on earth remained ignorant of one of the greatest dangers that has ever threatened the human race.

The next night, through the telescope of my astronomer friend Ogilvy, I saw the phenomenon with my own eyes. For the next ten nights, at exactly the same time, we and many other observers saw the same thing happen. A flaming mass heading towards earth, one each night.

Although I watched in fascination, I did not for one moment dream that Martians had fired missiles towards us, and that these missiles were now hurtling through space at thousands of miles a second, getting nearer and nearer. I did not even begin to consider that these flames would bring so much calamity and death to the earth. Each night, I returned home from Ogilvy's observatory to my comfortable home and my loving wife. Everything seemed so safe and tranquil.

Then came the night of the first falling star, a line of flame high up in the atmosphere. Below, hundreds of thousands of people in London and the Surrey countryside were sleeping in peace.

Convinced that a meteorite had landed on the common, Ogilvy rose early the next morning and strode out to investigate. On the grassy hillside, he found that a huge hole had been blasted violently into the earth, with sand and gravel flung in every direction. In places, the heather was on fire.

Then he saw the thing itself, half buried in the pit. It was a metal cylinder, more than thirty yards in diameter. Ogilvy knew that it could not be a meteorite. A noise came from within the cylinder. 'Good heavens,' said Ogilvy. 'There's someone in it. They must be half roasted to death and trying to escape!'

He rushed forward to help, but was beaten back by the great heat radiating from the cylinder. Unable to assist, he turned and ran wildly towards town. His route took him past the house where a journalist acquaintance, Henderson, lived.

'Henderson,' he called, 'you saw that shooting star last night?'

'Well?' said Henderson.

'It's out on Horsell Common now. But it's not a meteorite. It's a cylinder! And there's something inside. I'm wondering if it has anything to do with the Martian flares.'

Ogilvy told him all that he had seen.

Henderson was a minute or so taking it in, then snatched up his jacket. The two men hurried back to the common, and found the cylinder still lying in the same position. The sounds inside had ceased, and a thin circle of bright metal showed between the top and the body of the cylinder. Air was either entering or escaping at the rim with a thin, sizzling sound. They listened, rapped on the scaly burnt metal with a stick and, meeting with no response, concluded that whatever was inside must be dead. As they were unable to do anything more, they set off for town where Henderson went straight to the railway station in order to telegraph the story to London.

Word of mouth travelled even faster than the newspapers, and by eight that evening, a crowd had gathered by the pit to see 'the dead men from Mars'.

Early next morning I hurried down to the common. Quite a crowd had gathered, and Ogilvy and Henderson and several workmen were down in the pit with spades and pickaxes. They had uncovered a large portion of the cylinder, though its lower end was still embedded.

As I looked, I noticed movement at the end of the cylinder. Very slowly the circular top was rotating.

Ogilvy and the others scrambled from the pit. 'I say!' Ogilvy shouted. 'Keep back! We don't know what's in that confounded thing!'

The crowd around the pit now numbered some two or three hundred. As I watched, the end of the cylinder screwed all the way out and fell to the ground with a clang.

I saw something stirring within the shadows – greyish billows, and two luminous disk-like eyes. Then something resembling a grey snake coiled up, followed by another. A sudden chill came over me. There was a loud shriek from a woman behind me. As I began pushing my way back from the edge of the pit, I saw astonishment give place to horror on the faces of the people about me.

A grey, rounded bulk was crawling from the cylinder. Its skin caught the light, glistening like wet leather. Two large, dark eyes regarded the crowd. The thing's head was round, with a lipless, v-shaped mouth that quivered and panted and dribbled saliva.

Those who have never seen a living Martian can scarcely imagine the strange horror of its appearance. There was something fungoid in the oily brown skin, something unspeakably nasty in its clumsy movements.

Suddenly the monster vanished. It had fallen from the cylinder and dropped into the pit. I heard it give a low roar – and then I saw another creature appear in the mouth of the cylinder. I ran towards a stand of trees a hundred yards away. From there, I continued to watch the pit.

The sunset faded to twilight before anything further happened. Then I noticed a small knot of men advancing from the direction of the town, the foremost of whom was waving a white flag. I heard afterwards that there had been a hasty consultation, and since the Martians were evidently intelligent creatures, it had been resolved to show them, by means of the universally-recognised white flag, that we too were intelligent. Among the deputation were Ogilvy and Henderson.

Suddenly there was a flash of light, and a quantity of luminous greenish smoke came out of the pit in three distinct puffs. As the green smoke rose, the faces of those in the deputation flashed pallid green. Slowly a humped shape rose out of the pit, and the ghost of a beam of light flickered from it.

Then flashes of actual flame, a bright fire leaping from one to another, sprang from the scattered group of men.

It was as if some invisible jet landed on each in turn, flashing into white flame. By the light of their own destruction I saw them stagger and fall, and their supporters turning to run.

More beams of light flashed noiselessly from the pit, and people, pine trees, and even nearby houses were turned to flame. This flaming death, this invisible, inevitable sword of heat was sweeping the landscape. It was as if an intensely heated finger was being pointed by the Martians, destroying all in its path. I perceived it coming towards me by the flashing bushes it touched,

and was too astounded and stupefied to stir.
I watched the beam sweep towards me, then
stood up and ran madly, weeping like a child. I
did not dare look back. I remember feeling that,
even when I was on the verge of safety, this
mysterious 'heat-ray' might leap from the pit
and strike me down.

I remember nothing more of my flight except
the stress of blundering against trees and
stumbling through the heather. I arrived home
haggard and panting, burst into the dining
room and startled my wife. I sat down and
poured myself some wine,

and as soon as I had collected myself I told her the things I had seen. The dinner, which was a cold one, had already been served, and remained neglected on the table while I told my story.

Though still deeply shocked by what I had experienced, I sought not to frighten my dear wife. 'They may kill people who come near them, but I am convinced they cannot crawl from the pit. They are the most sluggish of creatures, and cannot move far or quickly on a planet whose gravity is three times that of Mars. But oh, the horror of them!'

'Please don't, dear,' said my wife, putting her hand on mine. I could see that her face was pale, and though my story might be hard to believe she was taking what I said deadly seriously.

'Poor Ogilvy!' I said. 'To think he is lying dead there.'

'What if they were to come here?' my wife said.

Remembering what Ogilvy had told me about the differences between the Martian environment and our own, I explained to my wife how both gravity and the thick atmosphere of earth were set solidly against the Martians. 'They have done a foolish thing,' I said, fingering my wine glass. 'They are dangerous only because they are mad with terror. Perhaps they expected to find nothing living on earth, certainly no intelligent living things who could easily defend themselves against Martian weapons.' With wine and food inside me, the confidence of being in my own home, and the necessity of reassuring my wife, I gradually felt more courageous and secure.

'One big shell in the pit,' I said. 'If the worst comes to the worst we can explode one big shell in the pit and kill them all.'

I did not know it then, but that was the last civilised dinner I was to eat for many strange and terrible days.

I slept badly that night and, rising early, decided to walk towards the common. I came across a company of soldiers, who told me that no one was allowed over the canal.

'Another cylinder fell last night, by all accounts,' said one soldier.

'We should crawl towards them under cover and rush 'em!' said another.

'What are they like?' a third soldier asked me.

I told him what I had seen.

'Octopuses!' said the soldier. 'It ain't no murder killing beasts like that!'

I left them and headed back into town, feeling better now that matters were in the hands of the military. I returned home, and at three o'clock I heard the sound of artillery fire. Later I found out that the pine wood, where the second cylinder had come down, was being shelled.

At six that evening, as I sat in the summerhouse with my wife, we heard a muffled detonation from the common. Almost immediately, as if in reply, we heard a crash, and I watched as the roof of a nearby house caved in. I gripped my wife's arm and rushed her into the road. 'We can't possibly stay here!' I said.

'But where can we go?' said my wife in terror.

'To my cousins in Leatherhead,' I said. I set off at once for the Spotted Dog, for I knew that the landlord had a horse and cart.

I gave that man two pounds, promising him that I would return the horse and cart at the earliest opportunity, and then returned home. We packed our bags and left the house. The trees at the bottom of the garden had been struck by the Martian heat-ray, and were on fire.

We climbed into the cart and I took up the reins. In seconds we were clear of the smoke and noise, and racing down the hill out of town.

We reached Leatherhead at nine o'clock and had supper with my cousins. At eleven I left my wife – her face was white with worry – and began the journey back. Had it not been for my promise to the innkeeper, I think she would have urged me to stay with her that night.

A storm began as I steered the cart, and on the western horizon I saw a blood-red glow, and masses of black smoke. As I approached the town I saw a light fall through the night and land in the east. It was the third falling star!

A minute later I saw something moving down the hill, perhaps half a mile away. How can I describe this monstrous thing? It was a tripod, higher than a house, a walking engine of glittering metal, and within it was one of the terrible octopus-like Martians. Seconds later a second tripod came crashing through the woods towards me – and I was galloping towards it!

I pulled on the reins, but the horse slipped, and a second later the cart overturned and I fell out into the road. I staggered to my feet and

moved to where the horse lay dead. I looked up.
The tripod was striding up the hill towards me. As
it passed, an exultant howl came from it – 'Aloo!
Aloo!' It was some moments before I could gather
myself and hurry on towards my house.

At last I reached home. I drank a shot of
whiskey and then changed my clothes. From the
window I looked out across the town. Martian
tripods moved busily to and fro. The town was
on fire, and several houses close by were in
ruins. Seconds later I saw a soldier stagger into
the garden. I leaned out of the window and
called to him.

'Come into the house!'

'My god!' he gasped as I drew
him in.

'Take some whiskey,'
I said.

He drank gratefully,
then sat down and began
to weep like a little boy.

'Wiped out!' he said at last. 'My artillery unit – all wiped out by the heat-rays! The Martians have destroyed the town – the railway station and the houses all about. I haven't seen a living soul—'

I calmed him, and made us a meal of bread and meat. Later, we sat by the window and stared out at the ruined town. Never before in the history of warfare had destruction been so indiscriminate. As we stared, three of the metallic tripods stood tall, their cowls rotating as though they were surveying the desolation they had created.

At dawn we decided to leave the house. My plan was to return to Leatherhead and to my wife. The problem was that the third Martian canister lay between us and Leatherhead, so I decided to make a detour north via Epsom. The artilleryman was heading for London, and we agreed to start our journey together.

After packing food and drink, we set off.
We hurried down the road, past dead bodies,
and entered the woods. There was not a breath
of wind, and everything was strangely still.
Of the Martians there was no sign.

Across a field we saw a line of cannon, with gunners standing beside them. 'That's good,' I said. 'At least they'll get a fair shot at the Martians.'

We arrived at Shepperton Lock, where we found a noisy crowd of refugees. There were far too many people for the ferries which crossed the River Thames.

'What's that?' someone said.

The sound came again, a muffled thud – the sound of a gun. The fighting had begun.

Seconds later the ground heaved underfoot and a heavy explosion shook the air.

'Here they are!' someone yelled.

Across the flat meadows, striding towards us, I made out four of the tripods. Then I saw a fifth – this one was carrying a deadly heat-ray and sweeping its fire over the town.

We stared in shocked silence for a second, until I cried, 'Get under the water!' I flung myself into the river and others did the same.

When I next looked, a tripod was wading across the river. At that moment cannons concealed on the far bank fired – and a shell hit the striding tripod! Damaged, the thing went striding off and blindly crashed into the tower of Shepperton church like a battering ram. Then at last the tripod, and the Martian within, lay still.

A violent explosion shook the air as the tripod's heat-ray fell into the river. A spout of water, steam and mud shot far into the sky. A wave of boiling water surged upriver, and I saw people screaming and shouting. Painfully scalded, I staggered through the hissing water towards the bank. I fell, and have a dim memory of a tripod's foot coming down a few yards from my head. When I looked up, I saw the four remaining tripods receding through the smoke. I knew that by some miracle I had escaped death.

Making my slow way towards London, I found an abandoned boat and rowed away from the destruction, past burning houses. I drifted for miles and at last came to Walton. There, sick with fever, I landed on the riverbank and lay down. I must have dozed, as I do not recall the arrival of the curate. I woke and became aware of a soot-smudged figure seated beside me. His eyes were large, pale blue, and stared blankly.

'What does it mean?' he trembled. 'I was out walking – and suddenly, fire, earthquake, destruction!'

I looked at him. It seemed that the ordeal had driven him almost mad.

'How can we escape?' he asked. 'They are invulnerable, pitiless.'

'Not invulnerable,' I said. 'I saw one killed just hours ago.'

He leapt to his feet. 'Listen!' he said.

We heard the distant noise of cannon fire and a remote, weird crying. The Martians had resumed their attack.

Later I learned what had happened during the following hours. Three Martian tripods had emerged from their pit and marched through the devastated town. Presently, they were joined by four other tripods, each carrying thick black tubes which they passed to the others.

Then the seven advanced, raising their tubes high and discharging canisters from them. These canisters smashed open upon striking the ground, and an enormous volume of inky vapour coiled out and spread slowly over the surrounding countryside. The touch of that vapour, the inhaling of its pungent wisps, was death to all creatures.

Before dawn the black vapour was pouring through the streets of London, and the poor Londoners were fleeing, or being gassed.

The curate and I were in Kew when we next saw a tripod. Night was falling, and far away across the meadows we made out four or five scurrying men and women pursued by a Martian tripod. It caught them up and, instead of using a heat-ray, plucked them one by one and tossed them into a metallic carrier.

We stood for a moment, petrified, and I wondered at the fate of my fellow humans. We set off again, sneaking along hedgerows and through plantations, watching keenly for the Martians.

Around midnight, we came to a deserted house within a walled garden. As neither of us had eaten in many hours, we were glad to find in the kitchen two loaves of bread and a leg of ham. There was even bottled beer.

We sat in the kitchen and ate hungrily. As we ate, there came a blinding glare of vivid green light. There followed a concussion, followed by a thud, and the ceiling came down upon us. I was knocked headlong across the floor and stunned.

We heard movement outside. 'What is it?'

'A Martian,' the curate whispered.

For hours we dared not move. Dawn came, and we saw through a gap in the wall a tripod standing sentinel over the still glowing cylinder which had demolished the rest of the house.

From outside there began a metallic
hammering, and then a violent hooting.
Presently we heard a measured thudding and a
vibration that made everything about us quiver.
For many hours we crouched there, silent and
shivering.

Through a small gap I could see daylight.
Slowly I made my way towards it and peered
out. The cylinder lay in a deep hole outside
the house, and next to it stood one of the great
tripods, stiff and tall against the sky. At first

I scarcely noticed the pit and the cylinder, because my attention was engaged by an extraordinary glittering mechanism, and the strange creatures that were crawling slowly and painfully across the heaped mound near it.

It was one of those structures that have since been called 'handling-machines', a metallic spider with five jointed, agile legs, and an extraordinary number of levers and clutching tentacles. Its motion was so swift, complex and perfect that at first I did not see it as a machine. The tripod fighting-machines were coordinated and animated to an extraordinary degree, but were nothing compared with this. The handling-machines behaved more like living crabs than machines.

My attention now turned to the Martians crawling around the glittering machine. They were the most unearthly creatures it is possible to conceive. Now I could clearly see their huge round bodies, each about four feet in diameter with a face in front of it. The face had no nostrils, but a pair of very large dark-coloured eyes, and just beneath this a kind of fleshy beak. Arranged around the mouth were sixteen slender whip-like tentacles, arranged in two bunches of eight.

Despite my desire to watch, fear drove me back into the kitchen. The curate was on his knees praying, after which he wept for hours. He ate more than I did; I pointed out that our only chance of survival was to remain in the house until the Martians moved on, so we would need to conserve our provisions.

Days passed, and the curate was at the peephole when the first humans were brought into the pit. He gestured to me, and I joined him. It was night-time, and little could be seen, though I thought I heard the murmur of human voices.

Then I saw a tripod, which reached behind and pulled something from the cage upon its back. The thing struggled violently, and only when it was placed upon the ground did I see that it was a man – I could see his staring eyes and gleams of light on his watch-chain.

For a moment there was silence, then I heard a terrible human shrieking, and a cheerful hooting from the Martians. It was only later that I fully understood what I was now seeing; that I understood how the Martians' digestive system needed to draw for their nourishment directly on the flesh of other species.

I covered my ears and scrambled from the peephole.

It was on the sixth day, in the darkness, that I heard the curate drinking in secret. We tussled over a bottle of burgundy he had discovered among the wreckage. I divided the remaining food, and would not let him eat any more that day.

In the afternoon he made another feeble effort to raid our provisions. He prayed and begged, and started to threaten me. He began to raise his voice.

'Shut up!' I hissed in terror, lest the Martian should hear us.

'No!' he shouted. 'I must speak! I must bear witness!'

He pulled away from me. Before he was halfway across the kitchen I took up a meat chopper hanging on the wall. In seconds I had overtaken him, and struck his head with the chopper's handle. He fell headlong and lay on the ground.

Suddenly I heard a noise outside.

I looked up and saw the tentacle of a handling-machine appear at the peephole, and then another. Through the gap in the wall I saw through the glass plate of the machine, and beheld the face of a Martian, its dark eyes peering. It was operating a metallic tentacle which snaked through the wreckage of the kitchen and touched the curate's head. I thought at once that it would notice the curate's wound and know that someone else was present.

The tentacle left the curate, and moved towards me. It touched my boot. I was on the verge of screaming, but I bit my lip, shaking with fear. For a moment the tentacle was still, and presently it withdrew.

I was thirsty and starving by now, and after many hours I overcame my fear and went in search of food. I found none, nor water. I was surprised to find that some fronds of red weed had grown across the hole in the wall, turning the light to the colour of blood.

I listened, but the pit was still and quiet. At last, encouraged by the silence, I crossed to the gap and looked out. There was not a living thing in the pit, save a few crows which picked at the bones of the men the Martians had consumed. I stared, hardly believing my eyes. All the machinery had gone.

I thrust myself through the red weed and stood on a mound of rubble, staring around me. The neighbouring houses had been wrecked, and the red weed grew over the ruins, weird and lurid like the landscape of another planet.

I moved on, struggling through the knee-deep weed. In a garden I found some young onions, and a quantity of immature carrots.

I continued towards London, through the riotous crimson weed.

I came to Putney, then Richmond, and saw that the valley of the Thames had become a red swamp. At sunset I came to the river. The whole area was desolate and silent.

I was later to learn that this red swamp was the final dying stage of the all-pervasive red weed, a weed which had come from Mars with the Martians, but had now succumbed to a terrestrial bacteria that destroyed it as quickly as it had at first flourished. Now the red weed rotted like a thing already dead. Its fronds became bleached, and then shrivelled and brittle. They broke off at the least touch, and the waters that had stimulated their early growth carried their last vestiges out to sea.

For a time I believed that humankind had been swept out of existence, that I was alone. Had the Martians exterminated everyone but myself?

I spent that night in a
tumbledown inn, and
in the morning found a rat-gnawed
crust and two tins of pineapple in a
nearby house. I ate ravenously.

Three things filled my mind: the killing of
the curate, the whereabouts of the Martians,
and the fate of my wife.

I told myself that I had had to keep the
curate quiet, and that I had not meant to
kill him. There were no witnesses. Then I
considered the Martians and the fate of my
wife, but about the Martians I had no idea, nor
had I any idea as to what might have become
of my wife.

I thought about what had happened to the
human race, and it came to me that the war
had taught us one thing, maybe – we now
might pity those witless souls, both human
and animal, which suffer at our hands.

I crossed the bridge over the river to Fulham. In a baker's shop I found bread – hard and mouldy, but eatable. I came upon dead bodies that had been there many days, and hurried on.

The further I moved on to London, the profounder grew the stillness.

In South Kensington I heard the first howling. It was a sobbing alternation of two notes, 'Ulla! Ulla!'

I moved on to Kensington Gardens, wondering at this strange, sad wailing. The large mansions were empty and still, and my footsteps echoed. Near the park gate I came upon an overturned bus, and the skeleton of a horse picked clean.

'Ulla! Ulla!' cried the voice, coming from the district of Regent's Park.

I was intensely weary and footsore. Why was I wandering in this city of the dead? I felt intolerably lonely. As I came to the top of Baker Street, I saw far away over the trees a Martian tripod, from which the strange howling came. I watched it for some time, but it did not move.

I pressed on towards Primrose Hill. I saw a second tripod, as motionless as the first, standing silently in the park. Suddenly the wailing ceased. The silence felt like a thunderclap.

On the summit of Primrose Hill I came upon a third Martian tripod, motionless like the others. An insane idea possessed me. Perhaps I should end my suffering now – what more was there to lose? I marched recklessly towards the tripod, and as I came closer I saw that a multitude of blackbirds was circling it.

I felt no fear as I ran towards the monster, only a wild trembling exultation. I stared up. From the hood on the top hung lank shreds of brown flesh, at which the hungry birds were pecking.

I looked about me from the top of the hill. All around I made out scattered tripods, handling-machines, and the bodies of more than fifty Martians. We now know, of course, that the Martians had been slain as the red weed had been slain, by bacteria found on earth that do not exist on Mars. After all man's devices had failed, the Martians had been felled by a humble bacterium.

These germs of disease have killed humans since life began on earth, but by virtue of natural selection we have developed resistance.

But there are no bacteria on Mars, and directly the Martians invaded, our microscopic allies began to work their overthrow.

For days I drifted through London, a man demented. When I came to, I found myself in a house of kindly people, who had found me on the third day wandering, weeping, and raving through the streets of St John's Wood. They have told me since that I was singing some insane doggerel about 'The Last Man Left Alive! Hurrah!'

Thanking them for their kindness, I now determined to make my way home. At Waterloo Station I found that a handful of trains were running again, and I sat in a carriage by myself and watched the sunlit scenes of devastation which passed the window. Woking station was undergoing repair, so I alighted at Byfleet and walked the rest of the way home. I passed the place where I had seen the first tripod, and found the broken cart and the whitened bones of the horse.

I came upon my house, and stumbled into the hall. I moved to my study, and found on my writing table the sheets of work I had left before the opening of the first Martian cylinder. I moved to the dining room. I found meat and bread, both far gone in decay. My home was desolate. 'It's no use,' said a voice in my head. 'The house is deserted. No one has been here for days. Do not stay here to torment yourself.'

I turned to the French window, which was
open. There, amazed and afraid, were my
cousin and my wife – my wife was pale and
tearful. She gave a faint cry.

'I came,' she said. 'I knew, I knew!'

She put her hand to her throat, swaying. I stepped forward and caught her in my arms.

Six years have now passed since the horrors I write of. I go to London from time to time, and watch the busy multitudes in Fleet Street and The Strand, like ghosts haunting the streets which I had seen silent and wretched. And strange, too, it is to stand on Primrose Hill, to see the people walking to and fro, to see the sightseers flocking around the Martian tripod that stands there still.

And strangest of all is to hold my dear wife's hand again, and to think that I counted her, and that she counted me, among the dead.

We have learned now that we cannot regard this planet as being fenced in and secure; we can never anticipate the unseen good or evil that may come upon us suddenly out of

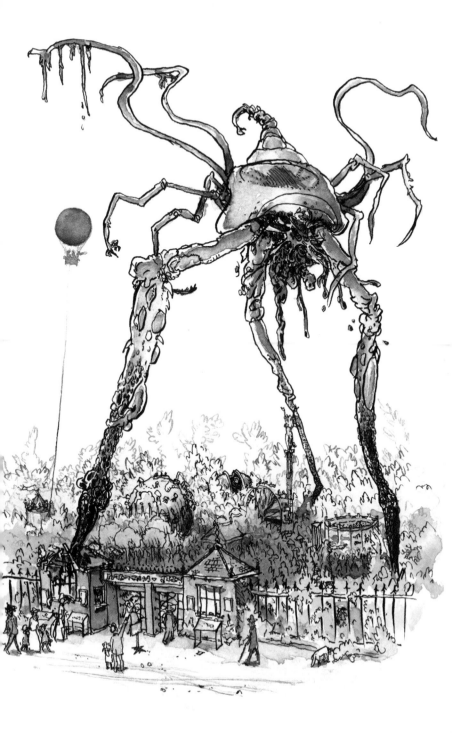

space. It may be that in the larger design of the universe this invasion from Mars is not without some benefit. It has robbed us of that serene confidence in the future which is the source of decadence. Its gifts to the advancement of human science are enormous, and it has shown us in the most dramatic fashion that all humankind must work together when faced by a universal threat.

TAKING THINGS FURTHER

The real read

This *Real Read* version of *The War of the Worlds*
is a retelling of H. G. Wells' magnificent work.
If you would like to read the full novel in all its
splendour, many complete editions are available,
from bargain paperbacks to beautifully-bound
hardbacks. You will be able to find a copy in your
local library or bookshop, or on the internet.

Filling in the spaces

The loss of so many of Wells' original words is a
sad but necessary part of the shortening process.
We have had to make some difficult decisions,
omitting sub-plots and details, some important,
some less so, but all interesting. We may also, at
times, have taken the liberty of combining two
events into one, or of giving a character words
or actions that originally belong to another. The
points below will fill in some of the gaps, but
nothing can beat the original.

- Wells describes the conditions on Mars in detail, and the narrator visits his friend the astronomer Ogilvy at his observatory. There they witness three points of light travelling from Mars, but the astronomer does not believe the planet has inhabitants who are signalling to us.

- We find out what is happening in London from the viewpoint of the narrator's younger brother. He hears about the invasion second-hand from newspapers, and witnesses the arrival of refugees from the fighting. Londoners panic as rumours spread of the poisonous black smoke.

- Londoners are desperate to flee the city, and people are trampled and crushed as they attempt to make their way to the railway stations. Train drivers refuse to return to the city, and the black smoke drives people north by bicycle, car, and on foot.

- The narrator's brother attempts to leave London, and manages to find a place on a steamship heading east. There he sees his first Martian tripods, which are striding along the coast destroying ships and boats. He watches as the guns of an ironclad warship bring down a tripod.

- The artilleryman takes the narrator to a house where he has been digging a great trench in order to reach the tunnels beneath London. The narrator sees the folly of this, and the folly of the artilleryman's grand plans to resist the Martians. Disgusted, the narrator leaves him and travels further into London.

- After seeing the damaged alien tripod on Primrose Hill, the narrator drifts, 'a demented man', for two days. Eventually he is taken in by kindly people, before setting off home. Towards the end of the story he speculates as to whether the Martians have also landed on Venus, and wonders whether they will attempt to return to our planet.

Back in time

H. G. Wells lived at a time of great change. Victorian Britain had a mighty empire and ruled much of the world. It had a vast army and navy, with which it defended its shores and subdued opponents around the world. Nevertheless, the Victorians worried about being invaded, and at the turn of the twentieth century popular literature reflected this, with hundreds of novels and short stories being published about invasions from Europe, particularly France and Germany.

Wells wanted to suggest that not only was the British Empire not invincible, but that planet earth itself might one day come under threat from another race fighting for its own survival. *The War of the Worlds* shows very clearly how fragile are our notions of society, culture and even humanity when threatened with the possibility of extinction.

Some people have claimed that the novel was a criticism of the way the British Empire ruled the world in Victorian times. In *The War of the Worlds*, they say, the Martians can be seen as the imperialists taking over land that was not theirs. As Wells was a socialist, who believed in equality among people and was opposed to British imperialism, this is possibly an accurate interpretation.

The War of the Worlds was one of the first novels about the earth being invaded by aliens. In Victorian times, not many people thought about the possibility of life on other planets – it was considered an impossibility that humankind might ever fly to the moon. Wells not only speculated about alien life on Mars, but he used the latest scientific knowledge to write about what life there might be like, and suggested that the inhospitable conditions on the 'red planet' were what prompted the Martians to invade earth.

Since Wells' time, many writers have written about alien invasion. Some writers have even continued the story of the Martian invaders, setting stories in different countries around the world. But not all science fiction stories are about evil invaders; many feature the arrival on Earth of peaceful extraterrestrials. Furthermore, a lot of science fiction is about how human beings travel to other planets – where they are the aliens. Wells himself wrote a novel, *The First Men in the Moon*, in which human space travellers journey to the moon and discover a race of insect-like Selenites.

Finding out more

We recommend the following books, websites and films to gain a greater understanding of H. G. Wells and the world he lived in.

Books

- H. G. Wells, *Selected Short Stories*, Penguin, 1989.

- J. D. Beresford, *H. G. Wells*, Dodo Press, 2007.

- Kevin J. Anderson, *War of the Worlds: Global Dispatches*, Bantam, 1996.

- Ann Kramer, *Victorians (Eyewitness Guides)*, Dorling Kindersley, 1998.

- John Christopher, *The Tripods Trilogy*, Puffin Books, 1984.

- Terry Deary, *Vile Victorians (Horrible Histories)*, Scholastic, 1994.

Websites

- www.hgwellsusa.50megs.com
The H. G. Wells Society website, with information about the author's life, his works and ideas.

- www.victorianweb.org

Interesting information about all aspects of Victorian life, including literature, history and culture.

- www.war-ofthe-worlds.co.uk

Comprehensive website about all aspects of *The War of the Worlds* – books, film, comics and much more.

- www.kirjasto.sci.fi/hgwells

A website all about books and writers, featuring essays on Wells and a full list of all his books.

- http://drzeus.best.vwh.net/wotw/wotw.html

A fascinating website about the publication of *The War of the Worlds* in countries around the world.

Films

- *The War of the Worlds,* directed by George Pal, 1953. This film is set in 1950s America, and is only loosely based on the novel. The Martians have flying machines, not tripods, but the ending in which the invaders succumb to earthly bacteria is the same.

- *The War of the Worlds,* directed by Stephen Spielberg, 2005.

Again, this version of the film is set in modern-day America, and follows a father who attempts to save his family from the invading Martians.

● In 1938 *The War of the Worlds* was made into a famous radio play by Orson Welles. Many people in America heard the broadcast and panicked when they thought that Martians were really invading Earth.

Food for thought

Here are some things to think about if you are reading *The War of the Worlds* alone, or ideas for discussion if you are reading it with friends.

In retelling *The War of the Worlds* we have tried to recreate, as accurately as possible, H. G. Wells' original plot and characters. We have also tried to imitate aspects of his style. Remember, however, that this is not the original work; thinking about the points below, therefore, can only help you begin to understand Wells' craft. To move forward from here, turn to the full-length version of *The War of the Worlds* and lose yourself in his science and imagination.

Starting points

- Why did the Martians decide to invade earth?

- Ogilvy the astronomer saw the 'falling star' – but what did he think it was?

- What was the reason for the narrator returning with the horse and cart to his home town?

- Which character do you find more interesting, the curate or the artilleryman? Why?

- Does anything in this novel frighten you? If so, why and how?

- What personal qualities do you see in the narrator?

- After thinking about what had happened to the human race, what does the narrator feel for those that suffer at the hands of humans?

- What is the narrator's reaction when he reaches Waterloo Station, and realises that the city is saved?

Themes

What do you think H. G. Wells is saying about the following themes in *The War of the Worlds*?

- invasion

- survival

- humanity

- destiny

- imperialism

Style

Can you find paragraphs containing examples of the following?

- descriptions of setting and atmosphere

- the use of simile to describe the Martians

- exclamation marks to add emphasis

- the use of imagery to enhance description

Look closely at how these paragraphs are written. What do you notice? Can you write a paragraph in the same style?